cloverleaf books™

Stories with Character

Yes I Can!
A Story of Grit

Mari Schuh

illustrated by Mike Byrne

M MILLBROOK PRESS • MINNEAPOLIS

For Dad, who taught me the
meaning of true grit —M.S.

For Harry, the 1st of many —M.B.

Text and illustrations copyright © 2018 by
Lerner Publishing Group, Inc.

Millbrook Press
A division of Lerner Publishing Group, Inc.
241 First Avenue North
Minneapolis, MN 55401 USA

For reading levels and more information, look up this title at
www.lernerbooks.com.

Main body text set in Slappy Inline 22/28.
Typeface provided by T26.

Library of Congress Cataloging-in-Publication Data

The Cataloging-in-Publication Data for *Yes I Can!: A Story of Grit*
   is on file at the Library of Congress.
ISBN 978-1-5124-8646-9 (lib. bdg.)
ISBN 978-1-5415-1071-5 (pbk.)
ISBN 978-1-5124-9825-7 (EB pdf)

LC record available at https://lccn.loc.gov/2017004730

Manufactured in the United States of America
1-43470-33210-6/27/2017

TABLE OF CONTENTS

Chapter One

A Big Project

Bzzzz! Dad's phone is buzzing.

"Your cousin Lisa's texting to say hi," Dad says. "Jada, do you want to text her back?"

"I'm in the middle of my science project," I say. "But tell Lisa I'll text her later!"

Lisa is one of my favorite people. But my project needs all my attention. I'm learning if plants grow best in water, milk, juice, or soda.

I've been working hard for four weeks.
I pour a liquid on each of my plants.

I measure how much the plants have grown. Then I write down what I find out in my science notebook.

It hasn't always been easy, but
I keep at it no matter what.

Mom and Dad say I have grit.

People with grit
work hard toward
long-term goals.

Ding-dong! The doorbell rings just as I'm writing in my science notebook. Who could it be?

Chapter Two
Staying Focused

"Jada, your friends
are here," Mom says.

"Can you play
with us?"
Diego asks.

I want to play, but I'm working on my plant project.

"Not today," I tell Diego. "But maybe I can play tomorrow."

Mom agrees. "Yes, tomorrow sounds good," she says.

"Ok!" Sara answers.

People with grit believe in themselves.

"Now do you think you'll be able to finish up your notebook entry?" Mom asks.

"Yes I can!" I tell her.

Chapter Three
Never Giving Up

I plan to finish my project today.
But I have a little trouble.
"No, kitty," I say. "Don't play with the plants!"

"Joey, **watch out!** You'll break the pot!"

"Orange juice! Yum!" says my sister.
"**Oh no!** That's for my project!" I tell her.

Dad starts getting dinner ready. He moves my things. "We need room for the dishes," he says.

"Wait!" I say. "The plants won't get sun if they aren't by a window. I'll move them to my bedroom window."

See my chart?
The plant that grew in water grew the best!

I did it! I'm done with my project.
I give it to my teacher, Mrs. Walton.
"How did it go?" she asks.

"Perfect!" I say. "Just perfect."

Make a Goals Journal

People with grit stay focused on their goals even when things are hard. Writing in a journal can help you reach your goals.

What You Will Need
a pencil
crayons or colored markers
a blank notebook or journal

What You Will Do

1) Write down some of your goals and dreams. What things do you want to do this year? Draw a picture of each goal and dream you want to achieve.

2) How will you make sure you reach your goals? Are there people who can help you?

3) Write down some ways it will be easier to reach your goals. Break down your goals into smaller steps.

GLOSSARY

chart: a sheet that gives information in the form of a table, diagram, graph, or picture

grit: the ability to work on long-term goals even when it's difficult

liquid: a wet substance that you can pour. Water, milk, juice, and soda are liquids.

project: an assignment worked on over a period of time

report: a document that gives information about something. A school report might give information about a student's research.

BOOKS

Johnson, Kristin. *In Your Shoes: A Story of Empathy.* Minneapolis: Millbrook Press, 2018. Read about another great quality to have: empathy, or the ability to imagine how someone else might feel.

Shepherd, Jodie. *Perseverance: I Have Grit.* New York: Children's Press, 2016. Learn how to keep going when things get tough.

Spires, Ashley. *The Most Magnificent Thing.* Tonawanda, NY: Kids Can, 2014. Follow along as a girl follows her dream to make the most magnificent thing—even when things don't quite go as planned.

WEBSITES

Character First Education: Determination
http://characterfirsteducation.com/c/curriculum-detail/2192365
Watch a video to learn more about determination.

Free Kids Crafts: Perseverance
http://www.freekidscrafts.com/cub-scout-coloring-pages/cub-scout
-coloring-page-perseverance
Complete a coloring page about never giving up.